KU-074-526

First published in Great Britain 2000
by Mammoth
an imprint of Egmont Children's Books Limited
239 Kensington High Street, London W8 6SA
10 9 8 7 6 5 4 3 2 1

Text by Elizabeth Laird ©
Egmont Children's Books Limited 2000
Illustrations copyright © Simone Lia 2000

ISBN 0 7497 3817 0

A CIP catalogue record for this title is available from the British Library

Printed in Hong Kong.

This paperback is sold subject to the condition
that it shall not by way of trade or otherwise,
be lent, resold, hired out, or otherwise circulated
without the publisher's prior consent in any form
of binding or cover other than that in which
it is published and without a similar condition
including this condition being imposed
on the subsequent purchaser.

STANDARD LOAN

UNLESS RECALLED BY ANOTHER READER
THIS ITEM MAY BE BORROWED FOR

FOUR WEEKS

TO RENEW, TELEPHONE:
01243 816 089 (BISHOP OTTER)
01243 816 099 (BOGNOR REGIS)

12. FEB 03.   18. FEB 07.

22. FEB 01.   02. APR 03.
               08. SEP   10. APR 07.
29 APR 01.

-1 JUN 2001   03 NOV 03.   04. NOV 07.

NOV 01.   07. DEC 03.   16. DEC 07.

DEC 01.   MAR 04.   27. MAY 08.

                          14. NOV 08.

11 FEB 02   1 2 NOV 2009
                          18 JAN 2010

SEP 04
04. DEC 06.

WITHDRAWN

Little to

Goldilocks and the Three Bears

Elizabeth Laird
illustrated by Simone Lia

picture mammoth

UNIVERSITY COLLEGE CHICHESTER LIBRARIES

AUTHOR:
LAIRD

WS 2169579 2

TITLE:
THREE

CLASS NO:
P/LAI

DATE:
12-2000

SUBJECT:
CR

The Three Little Pigs

Once upon a time there were three little pigs who went out into the world to seek their fortunes.

The first little pig met a man who was carrying a load of straw. "Please will you give me some of your straw," the little pig asked most politely, "so that I can build myself a house?"

"Very well," the man said.

So the little pig built himself a beautiful house of straw.

By and by a big bad wolf came along, and when he saw the little pig in his little straw house, he wanted to eat him for his dinner. So he called out, "Little pig, little pig, let me come in!"

But the little pig answered, "No no, by the hair of my chinny chin chin, I will not let you in."

Then the big bad wolf was cross and he said,
"Then I'll huff and I'll puff and I'll blow your house in!"

So he huffed and he puffed, and the house of straw came tumbling down, and the big bad wolf ate the little pig for his dinner.

The second little pig met a man who was carrying some sticks. "Please will you give me some of your sticks," the little pig asked very politely, so that I can build myself a house?"

"Of course I will," the man said.

So the little pig built himself a beautiful house of sticks.

By and by the big bad wolf came along, and when he saw the second little pig in his little house of sticks, he wanted to eat him for his tea. So he called out, "Little pig, little pig, let me come in!"

But the little pig answered, "No no, by the hair of my chinny chin chin, I will not let you in."

Then the big bad wolf was even crosser and he said, "Then I'll huff and I'll puff and I'll blow your house in!"

So he huffed and he puffed, and he huffed and he puffed and the house of sticks came crashing down, and the big bad wolf ate the little pig for his tea.

The third little pig met a man who was carrying a load of bricks. "Please will you give me some of your bricks," the third little pig asked extremely politely, "so that I can build myself a house?"

"Certainly," the man replied.

So the little pig built himself a beautiful house of bricks.

By and by the big bad wolf came along, and when he saw the little pig in his beautiful house of bricks, he wanted to eat him for his supper. So he called out, "Little pig, little pig, let me come in!"

But the little pig answered, "No no, by the hair of my chinny chin chin, I will not let you in."

Then the big bad wolf was very cross and he said, "Then I'll huff and I'll puff and I'll blow your house in!"

So he huffed and he puffed, and he huffed and he puffed, and he *huffed* and he *puffed* but the house of bricks did not fall down, and the big bad wolf had nothing to eat for his supper.

The big bad wolf thought of a trick to catch the little pig. "Little pig," he said, "come to the field with me at six o'clock tomorrow morning, and we'll dig up some turnips together."

The little pig liked turnips so he agreed. Next morning he got up at five o'clock, and was safe home again with a sackful of turnips by the time the wolf arrived at the turnip field.

The wolf was very, very cross, but he soon thought of another plan. "Little pig," he said, "come to the orchard with me at five o'clock tomorrow morning, and we'll pick some apples together."

The little pig liked apples so he agreed, but next morning he got up at four o'clock and climbed an apple tree and started picking apples.

But this time the wolf had come early too, and he was soon standing at the bottom of the apple tree, licking his lips, and hoping to eat the little pig for his breakfast.

The little pig pretended to be glad to see the big bad wolf and he threw him an apple. While the wolf was picking it up, he scrambled down from the tree, and climbed into a barrel. Then he rolled himself all the way home as quickly as he could, and ran in and shut the door, and the wolf wasn't fast enough to catch him.

The big bad wolf was furious that the little pig had tricked him, and he climbed up onto the roof of the house. I'll climb down the chimney, he thought, and catch him that way.

But the little pig had lit a big fire and put a cauldron of water to boil on it.

When the wolf came down the chimney, he fell with a splash and a hiss into the boiling water. The little pig quickly put the lid on the cauldron, and that was the end of the big bad wolf.

As for the little pig, he lived happily ever after in his little brick house.

Goldilocks and
the Three Bears

Once upon a time there were three bears who lived in a house in the woods. Father Bear was a great big bear. Mother Bear was a middle-sized bear, and Baby Bear was a tiny little bear.

One morning, their porridge was too hot, so the three bears went out for a walk in the woods to give it time to cool. And while they were out, a little girl called Goldilocks walked past their house.

Goldilocks peeped in through the window.

No one was there.

So she opened the door and went inside.

No one was there.

She looked right round the house.

No one was there.

Goldilocks saw the porridge cooling on the table. She was hungry so she tried some from Father Bear's great big bowl. It was too hot. Next she tried some from mother Bear's middle-sized bowl and that was too cold. So she tried some from Baby Bear's tiny little bowl. It was just right, and Goldilocks ate it all up.

Then Goldilocks wanted to sit down, so she sat down on Father Bear's great big chair. It was too hard. She sat down on Mother Bear's middle-sized chair. It was too soft. She sat down on Baby Bear's tiny little chair. It was just right, but Goldilocks was too heavy for the little chair, and it broke – snap! crack!

Next Goldilocks felt sleepy so she went upstairs to find a bed. She tried Father Bear's great big bed, but it was too high. She tried Mother Bear's middle-sized bed, but it was too low. Then she tried Baby Bear's tiny little bed. It was just right, and Goldilocks climbed right into it and went to sleep.

A little while later, the three bears came home to eat their porridge. They went to the table, sat down and lifted up their spoons.

"Who's been eating my porridge?" said Father Bear in his loud, growly voice.

"Who's been eating my porridge?" said Mother Bear in her soft, gentle voice.

"Who's been eating my porridge?" said Baby Bear, in his little squeaky voice, "because whoever it is, they've eaten it all up!"

Then the three bears looked at their chairs.

"Who's been sitting on my chair?" said Father Bear in his loud, growly voice.

"Who's been sitting on my chair?" said Mother Bear in her soft, gentle voice.

"Who's been sitting on my chair?" said Baby Bear in his little, squeaky voice, "because whoever it is, they've broken it!"

Then the three bears went upstairs. Father Bear looked at his bed. The pillow was all squashed.

"Someone's been sleeping in my bed," he said, in his loud, growly voice.

Mother Bear looked at her bed. The quilt was all rumpled.

"Someone's been sleeping in my bed," she said, in her soft, gentle voice.

Baby Bear looked at his bed, and saw a golden head lying on the pillow.

"Someone's been sleeping in my bed," he said, in his little, squeaky voice, "and she's *still here*!"

Now Goldilocks was fast asleep, and Father Bear's loud, growly voice sounded like distant thunder. Mother Bear's soft, gentle voice sounded like water in the stream falling over stones, but Baby Bear's little, squeaky voice sounded as loud and clear as a whistle, and it woke Goldilocks up.

When Goldilocks opened her eyes and saw the three bears looking at her, she had such a terrible fright that she gave a great scream. She jumped out of bed, scrambled out of the window and ran all the way home.

And the three bears never saw Goldilocks again.